D1063161

To Lauren,

MERRY
CHRISTMAS!

GRAHAM

Christmas Eve is the hardest night of the year to fall asleep.

Copyright 2014
by Little Black Book Press.

ISBN: 0-9672865-9-X
All rights are reserved.
No part of this book maybe
used or reproduced in any
manner without written
permission from the author.

To contact the author or order copies:
Go to: www.LeosOtherChristmas.com
Email: graham@grahamsale.com

Leo's Other Christmas

Written and Illustrated by
Graham Sale

Published by Little Black Book Press

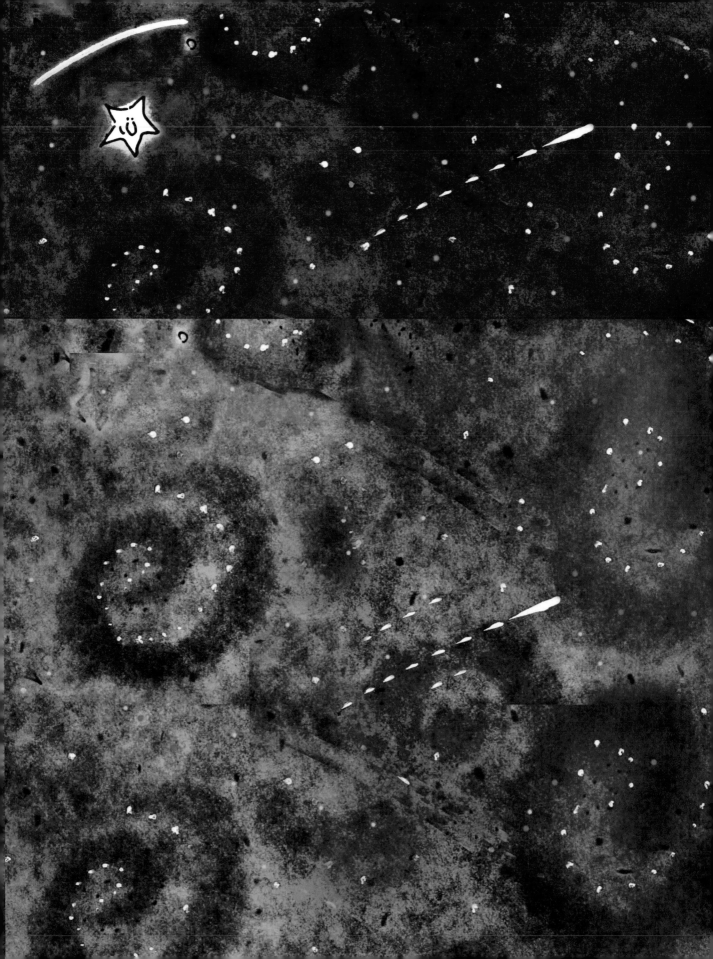

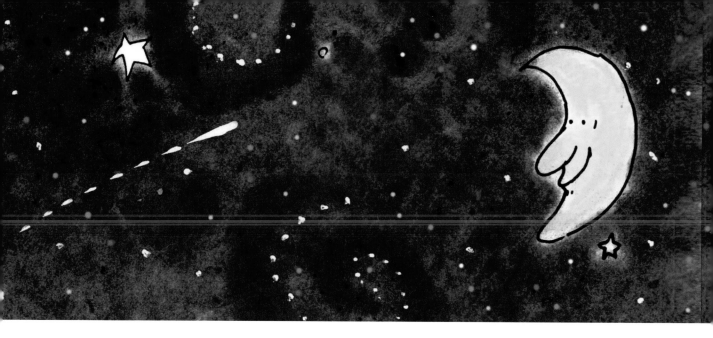

It seemed like it took Christmas forever to arrive. But tonight was finally Christmas Eve.

Like every Christmas Eve, Leo and his family climbed in their car and drove through town to look at the sparkling lights and holiday decorations, adorning peoples' homes. The night was magical.

The snowy streets twinkled with Christmas colors. Each house seemed more beautiful than the last. Leo especially liked it when they stopped to listen to Christmas carolers. Their voices transformed the stillness, making the night even more wondrous.

As the evening grew late, Leo and his family returned home. They snuggled into their beds and waited for Christmas morning to come at last.

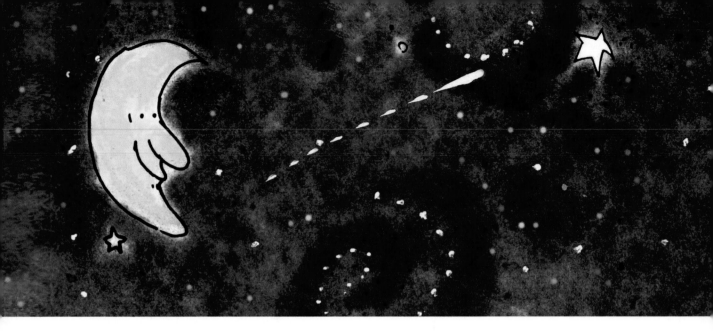

As Leo's parents tucked him into bed and kissed him goodnight, his father said,

"You know it might be a good idea if you tried to get some sleep before morning, son."

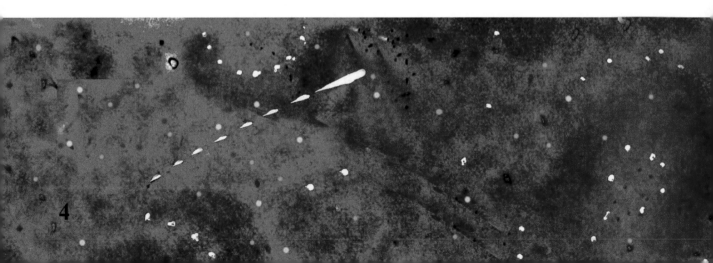

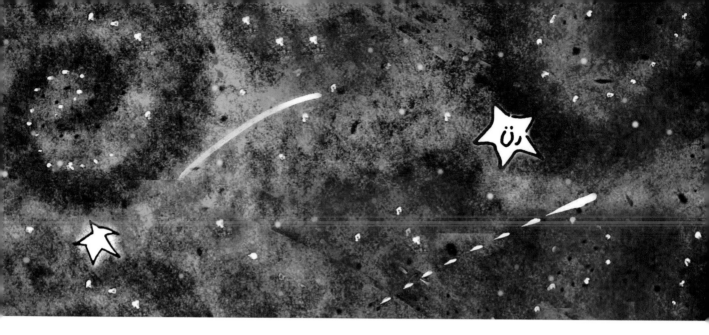

Leo smiled and
closed his eyes.

Christmas Eve was
the hardest night
of the year to
fall asleep.

Leo's head was filled
with thoughts of all the gifts

that would be waiting for him
under his family's Christmas tree.

He made a list and circled everything he wanted in the Wish Book catalog that arrived in the mail.

His mother didn't want him to read it
and threw it in the wastebasket.
But Leo found it and saved it.

He hid the Wish Book under his bed
and took it out when he was alone.

He spent hours and hours looking through it.

There were more toys
in that Wish Book than
he ever imagined existed
in the whole world.

And he wanted almost
all of them!

Sometimes though,

he felt disappointed and even angry
on Christmas morning

when he opened his presents and
found that he didn't get everything
he wished for.

Still, it was exciting

just waiting
and hoping.

Leo tossed and turned until
he finally drifted off to sleep.

Suddenly,
from a deep sleep, Leo was awakened by
the sound of his door opening softly.
A dark figure entered his room and
moved silently towards his bed.

"Leo. Leo, wake up," the voice said.
He recognized the voice.
It was his mother.
"Leo dear, wake up. I need to talk with you."

"What time is it?" he asked sleepily.

"It's still very early," she replied.
"Not nearly time to get up yet."

"What's the matter?", Leo asked.

"I need your help, dear.

"As you know, your father and I work with the Arctic League. The League collects and delivers toys to very poor families who sign their names to a list. They have no money Leo, and without these toys their children would have no Christmas.

"But I just received a call from the main office. There was a mistake. One family was forgotten.

"They signed the list but didn't receive any toys. These children, who are younger than you Leo, have no father. And their mother promised them that Santa would not forget them."

"Now Leo, I need you to help me.
Go up into the attic and pick out
some toys of your own, enough for three
children. Do you understand what I'm
asking you to do?" his mother asked.

There was a big lump in his throat, and
Leo couldn't speak. He just nodded his
head yes.

"Fine, there's no time to waste.
It will be morning soon, so we must hurry.
Get the toys and meet me in the car."

Leo took a deep breath, put on his robe
and slippers and headed up to the attic.

It was hard to give away toys he still liked.

Neither Leo nor his mother spoke
in the car as they made their way
through the dark, snowy night
to the other side of town.

As they crossed the railroad tracks,
everything changed.

There were no Christmas lights on
these houses. Many had boards on
their windows. And some had
no windows at all.
It was scary.

Finally, they turned onto
a small side street and stopped.

His mother's voice broke the silence.
"That's the house, Leo."

He looked across the street. It didn't look
like anybody could live in a house like that.
He heard dogs barking. Leo shivered.
It felt dangerous.

"Leo, I…I know it's hard," his mother began,
"but I want you to take the toys into them."
Leo didn't want to. He was frightened.
This was all too serious. He was just a little boy.
If this was so important, why couldn't
his mother do it?

"But, what will I say?" he protested.
"You can tell them you are Santa's helper, Leo."

Leo wanted to argue. But when he looked into
his mother's eyes, he knew he had to go.

17

Leo reached into the back seat,
grabbed the sack of toys and
stepped out into the cold, dark night.

The deep snow spilled over the
tops of his boots as he slowly
made his way towards the house.

The freezing wind swirled around him.
Suddenly, a strong gust snatched
his hat away.

Finally he reached the house and stopped
at the steps leading to the front door.

He wanted to run back to the car
and make his mother take
them home.

But he started up the steps instead.
Each step creaked with his weight.

Suddenly, with a loud CRACK,
a step splintered beneath his foot,
and he fell through up to his knee.

Leo's heart pounded in his throat!

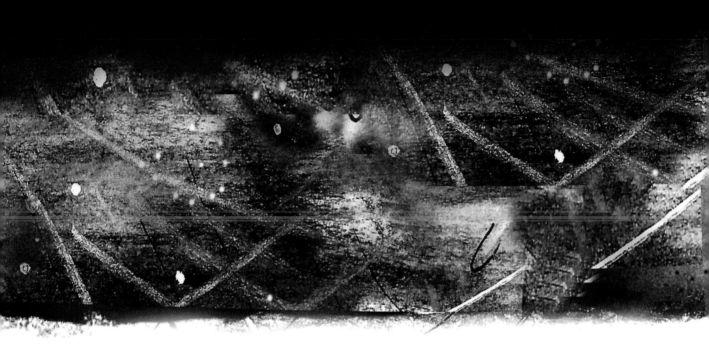

Leo quickly pulled his foot back out
from between the boards and leapt up
the final two steps to the front door.

But there wasn't a door.
Well, there was,
but it looked broken.
A large piece of wood was nailed to it.
Cardboard and plastic bags were
taped across the frame to keep
out the cold.

The strong wind had torn
most of the plastic loose, and
the cardboard was soggy and wet.

He was scared and wanted to turn
and run away, but he knocked instead.

A woman answered the door.
She looked like a girl.
She was much younger than his mother.
Her hair wasn't combed, and she was
wrapped in a blanket.

Her eyes were swollen and red.
Leo could tell she'd been crying.
He was embarrassed and looked down.

That's when he saw her bare feet
on the frozen door step.

All this happened so quickly that he wasn't aware that she had pulled him into the house and closed the door behind him.

The room was empty except for a stuffed chair, which was torn and missing a leg. A bare bulb dangled from the ceiling, casting a harsh light on the yellowed walls. It was almost as cold inside the house as it was outside, and it smelled unclean.

There was a small, low table, two metal chairs and a stained, striped mattress that lay on the cold bare floor with three little children sitting on it. They were huddled together under a blanket sobbing.

Then his eyes fell on some branches,
Christmas tree branches. He glanced back
across the empty room. He hadn't noticed a tree.
Then he realized that was their Christmas tree.

"What do you want?" the mother asked.

"I, I…I was outside just now, walking down
the street. And at the end of the block, I saw a
man in a sleigh. He was stuck in the snow and
he called me over to help him." Leo's voice
became stronger and more confident. The children
stopped crying and listened as Leo spoke.

"He said that he had one more delivery to make
before morning, to some children who lived on
this block. And since he was stuck he asked me
to deliver his gifts for him."

"So…these are for you."

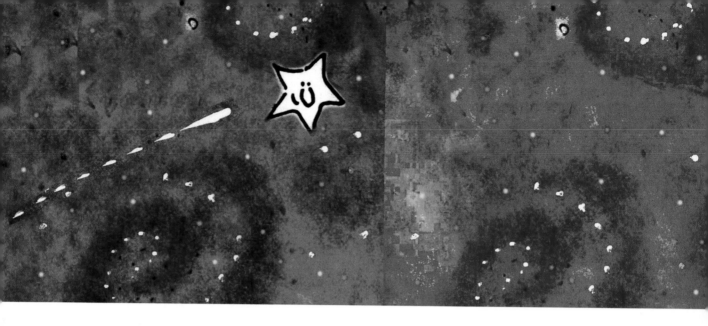

As soon as Leo put the sack down on
the floor, the children ripped it open.
They pulled out the toys and cried,
"Santa came! He came! He didn't forget us!"

Leo stepped back and
felt for the door behind him.

He looked at the mother.
Tears were running down her cheeks.
Her lips trembled as she moved her mouth
to speak. But no sound came out.

Leo could see *gratitude* in her eyes.

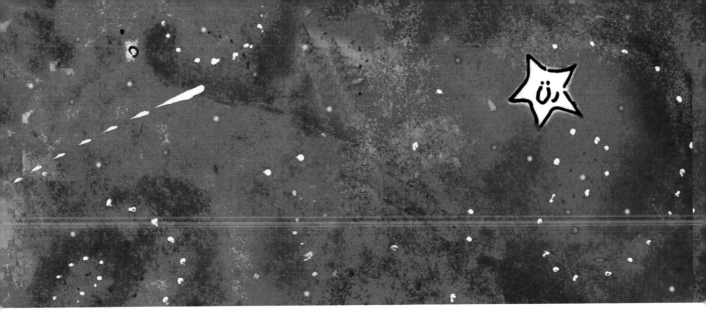

He turned to leave.

Then he turned around
again and took off his scarf
and gave it to her.

"Merry Christmas,"
he said softly.

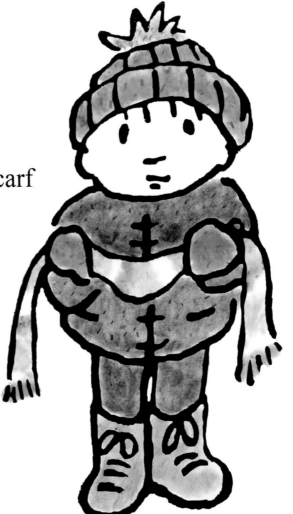

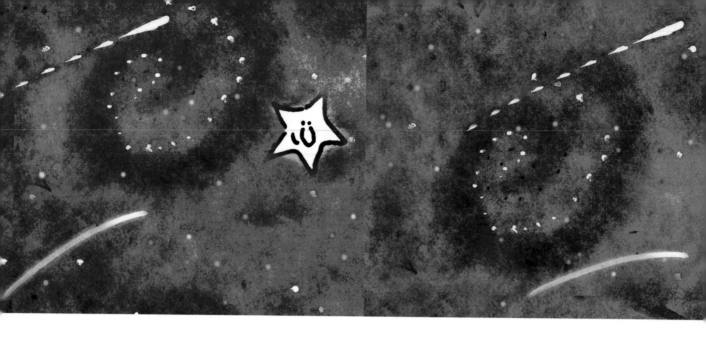

Leo and his mother were quiet
on the way home.

When they walked into the house,
Leo's mother turned to him and said,

"Thank you, dear.
I'm proud of you for doing that.
We still have a few hours before it's time
to get up. I'll see you in the morning,"

She kissed her son and
went upstairs to her bedroom.

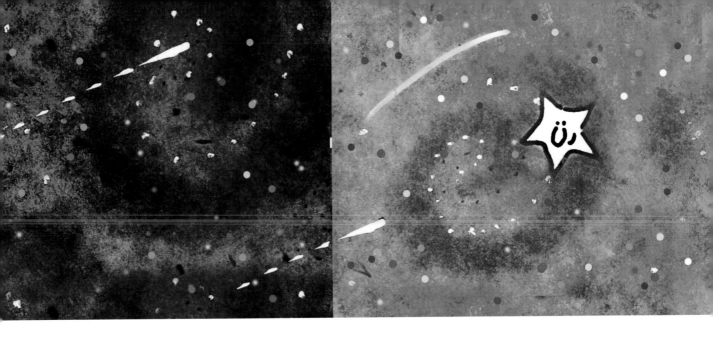

Leo started up the stairs,
and then turned and looked
back down into the living room
at their Christmas tree.

In a little while, his father would
come down and turn on its lights.

But to Leo,
it already was
shining brightly.

THE END

To contact the author or order copies:

Visit: www.grahamsale.com
Email: graham@grahamsale.com

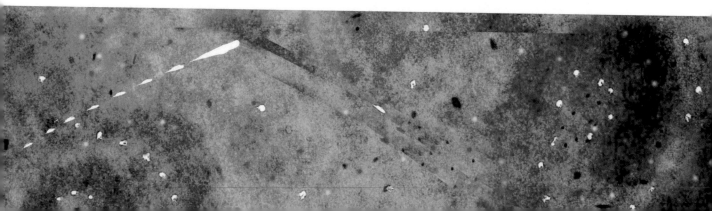

Author's Note

This based on a true story that happened to me when I was ten years old.

I am forever grateful to my mother for waking me that cold Christmas morning to let me experience the true meaning of the holiday for myself. Isn't that the way the best lessons are learned?

Thank you mom.

36451896R00022

Made in the USA
Columbia, SC
25 November 2018